D0005135

Field Day!

Story by Samantha Margles
Illustrated by the Disney Storybook Artists

DISNEY PRESS

New York
An Imprint of Disney Book Group

Manufactured in China.
Conforms to ASTM F963-07 and EN71.

Library of Congress Catalog Card Number on file

First Edition

10 9 8 7 6 5 4 3 2 1

For more Disney Press fun, visit www.disneybooks.com

The toys were gathered in Andy's room. Andy was at school, so they had decided to have a field day. The Little Green Aliens had promised to teach the toys new games.

Buzz Lightyear was eager to start. He flew above them, a big smile on his face. "To the games!" he cried.

Woody was so excited that he jumped up and yelled "Yeeehaaah!"

The Little Green Aliens stood in front of the television.
They wanted to show a video about one of the games.
The video showed Buzz playing Zipaway.
"Ooo," said one Little Green Alien.
"Ahhh," said the second Little Green Alien.

Now the video showed Jessie chasing after Buzz. Some of the toys started to get nervous. The game looked hard!

"Don't worry. Zipaway is fun!" said one Little Green Alien. "Now, let's try it!"

The aliens picked Slinky to be the Zipper. He chased the other toys around until he caught one. Then that toy became the Zipper.

The Little Green Aliens were right. The game was fun!

After the toys finished playing Zipaway, the Little Green Aliens brought out some cereal puffs.

"Let's play Blammball," one Little Green Alien said.

"We throw the Blammballs, and you try not to get hit!" said the second Little Green Alien.

"Ready, set, go!" the Little Green Aliens shouted together.

The Little Green Aliens began to throw the Blammballs. The toys all did their best not to get hit. Rex tried to catch them with a baseball mitt. Hamm jumped on top of a Blammball. Slinky ran away from the Blammball as fast as he could!

When the Little Green Aliens took a break, the toys all stopped to catch their breath.

"That was great!" Hamm exclaimed. "What else can we play?"

The Little Green Aliens marched to the center of the room.
"It is time to play a game with music," one of them said.
"To the record player!" cried Buzz.

The toys all gathered around the record player. Woody turned it on, and the record started to spin.

"This is Spinnorwhip," said a Little Green Alien. "You must run on the spinning disk without falling."

The toys had fun trying to run on the record, but they kept falling down—even Bullseye!

"Let's begin Bubble Bandeeni!" said one Little Green Alien. The goal was to catch a bubble and hold it for as long as they could. The toy with the last bubble won!

While Woody blew bubbles, the toys ran around and caught them. Buzz's bubble was so big he could see himself in it!

The toys played new games for most of the day. Andy would be home soon, but there was one thing left to do.

"This is the best part of field day!" said one Little Green Alien. "Now we dance!"

The toys cheered and danced until they heard Andy running up the stairs. Field day had been lots of fun!